A SERIES OF DREAMS

A SERIES OF DREAMS

TONY MARTIN

authorHOUSE®

AuthorHouse™
1663 Liberty Drive
Bloomington, IN 47403
www.authorhouse.com
Phone: 1-800-839-8640

First published by AuthorHouse   09/14/2011

ISBN: 978-1-4567-9842-0 (sc)
ISBN: 978-1-4567-9879-6 (ebk)

Printed in the United States of America

Any people depicted in stock imagery provided by Thinkstock are models, and such images are being used for illustrative purposes only.
Certain stock imagery © Thinkstock.

This book is printed on acid-free paper.

Because of the dynamic nature of the Internet, any web addresses or links contained in this book may have changed since publication and may no longer be valid. The views expressed in this work are solely those of the author and do not necessarily reflect the views of the publisher, and the publisher hereby disclaims any responsibility for them.

for my two sons

shane & alan

and bob dylan for the inspiration

a Brighter Life

by Tony Martin on Apr 19. © TONY MARTIN,

It should have ended
but still it drags on,filled with silence,
CRUSHING,
waiting for the dawn,
the pressure eases
darkness begins to fade
BREATHE EASY
as the light breaks through the shade.
A new day drifts by
floating in with the dew
bringing release from the nightmares
since losing you.
The warmth from the sun
disguises the heartfelt anguish,
CRUSHING,
waiting,for the reason,
longing for the truth
to explain the treason
that feeds the nightmares
that linger through the darkness
long into the dawn.
As the daylight progresses once more towards the torment
of self induced torture,
trying to release you from the love
only I could feel,
slowly the night approaches
once again drifting into the darkness
CRUSHING,
waiting for the nightmare's return.
The night's grow longer as the years pass by,
sometimes the feelings grow weaker

as the nightmare begins,
holding on to a dream
through life's tormented sins,
DEEPER,DEEPER,
the nightmare grips my mind
replaying your words on that cold dark night
when your heart became unkind.
Destroying plans
for a future full of promise and hope
were we too young?
not experienced enough to cope?.
So now I must decide
the time has come to let go
to release you from the promise you made
all those years ago,
nightmares in the darkness of despair
reliving the pain of a love so deep
you could not share.
Now the night is over
dawn rolls in with the dew,
decision is made
ending the torment of a promise spoken by you.
Pleasant dreams now
from this day,
will fill the night with softer darkness
drawing me into a life of happiness,
no more penalties to pay.

TONY MARTIN 19/4/2011

a Different View

by Tony Martin on Nov 8, 2010. © TONY MARTIN,

Through circles of clear white light
You smile
Showing the loveliness of life
Through the jealousy and hatred
Of someone less important than the sand
It took to make the glass you now see through.

TONY MARTIN 11-9-1997

a Good Man

No curtains at the windows
Coats on the bed,
Wife is hungry,kids to be fed,
Sackcloth and ashes
Shortage of food,
Can't find any work
No matter how good.

Is it right we should suffer
Whilst you live as you do?

Seems like a lifetime
Just waiting in this line,
What happens at the end if they don't give
What you need
Will our kids remain hungry
As they continue to feed.?

Is it right we go hungry
Whilst you feed as you do.?

No fuel for the fire
Hope it don't snow,
Are the kids warm enough?
Hope my anger don't show,
I can't help it,believe me I try
Sometimes the effort seems so futile
Makes me want to cry.

Why can't you suffer
Whilst we live as you do.?

4

Would it really help,
Would anything change?
If we swapped places
But kept the same name
Would your wealth do me good?
I don't think that it would,
So I will stay as I am
And remain a GOOD MAN.

TONY MARTIN 16-8-1996

a Lonely Thought

To quench this thirst of longing
with the nectar of togetherness,
the warmth from your breasts
I feel as your desire
enfolds my chest.
A feeling no longer wasted
as your lust for me takes over,
Heaven at last to be tasted
as you take me for your lover,
two lips of silken kisses
breathing sighs of wanton lust,
after a lifetime of tragic misses
at last a love to trust.
Dining slowly on the fruits ofCupid
as the darts of love sink deeper,
savour the hunger which too long
lingered in the heart of this lonely sleeper.
Awaken these desires as you
take me to your breast,
the fullness of your charms
put my eager body to the test,
my hands with trembling fervour
trace a path towards your soul
eagerness and longing cause sensations
beyond my control as you give yourself
willingly to one who had forgotten
how to make a woman feel whole.
The warmth of womanly wonders
seeping slowly through your skin,
your breasts heaving rhythmicaly
with the heat from within,

as my lips encircle the buds of
womanhood drawing life
from your soul,
your knees now astride me
your breasts fill my eyes
allowing the honey from your body
to flow between your thighs,
ever closer you allow me to search
with my hand,
guiding nervously my manhood
towards the promised land.
Entering slowly,afaid to rush,
eagerness takes over
with one final push
through the entrance into Heaven
releasing the past,accepting the future
now everything is given.
The release of painful emotion
flowing as tides to the shore
the fear of loneliness gone
tears of longing no more.
The final act of love as your
Garden of Eden reaches my mouth
and I savour the first taste
from your fountain of youth,
then the slow descent from ecstasy
as your mouth locks on to mine
tongues searching for the honey to share sealing the love that is created
when two bodies entwine.

a Prayer for Debra

To be near you in thought
only in my mind,
you allow me your wisdom
you are so very kind.
From across this majestic pond
your words to me fly,
my thoughts of you remain fond
as they soar through God's heavenly sky.
Accept these words of admiration
from a friend far away,
loaned to me through God's creation
to guide you through your day.
Your faith in God inspires me
this I wish I could share,
sometimes the pain I feel
causes me not to care.
Then your words of love and hope surround me
returning light into this grave,
caressing me with wonderful feelings
and hope that one day
my soul he will save.

TONY MARTIN. 28-05-2011.

BEER CELLAR BLUES
(*wendy's song*)

"Help us to find the owner of this car,somebody move it
The night closes in and our journey is far"

Search the Club,nobody leave
Open every door
But wait,don't go in the cellar
That would cause the lovers to grieve.

Over the barrell was once the bosses favourite position
But wait,all you need now is
A green shirt,a pleated skirt and an itchy disposition.

"Help us to find the owner of this car,somebody move it
The night closes in and our journey is far"

You will just have to wait I can't CUM yet
But wait,one final push,nearly there
Won't be long,don't fret.

At last it's over we can all go home
She is done with her lover,made his bell ring
But wait,is there still more
There must be,It was just his mobile phone.

"Help us to find the owner of this car,somebody move it
The night closes in and our journey is far"

TONY MARTIN 15-6-1997

Chase the Moon

by Tony Martin on Feb 15. © TONY MARTIN,

As we drove through the descending gloom
Across the horizon she rose
The glowing moon,
An air of fascination came over you
For this object in the night sky,
"Would you like to hold her"Iasked,
As she slowly drifted by.
"This is not the man I once knew "you thought
As we turned towards this fascinating glow,
Across the horizon she drifted
Enticing us to follow.
So close,Almost in reach,Waiting to be held
As if a lesson to teach.
My hand you held as we followed the moon
Releasing the warmth of her spleandour,
As she drifted away,smiling softly at you
Whispering gently,
"Take your time,love will shine through"

TONY MARTIN 16-02-2011.

CLOUD DANCER
(A week in the life of a comet)

by Tony Martin on Mar 10, 2010.

Raindrops,snowflakes
Thunder in the sky,
Even the moon shines brighter
But no one knows why.

Faster than sound
Yet visually still,
No clouds to cover where you are bound
Or to change your will.

Darkness surrounds
The light you show,
The devastation you will cause
Only you know.

Silently you pass through the sky.
Stirring up thoughts of
Times and situations
Which have passed us by.

Harsh wind and cold rain
Surround me tonight,
Bringing me comfort
Instead of fright.

When you return
Another mind will seek the truth,
Until then you will travel through this universe
And remain so aloof.

TONY MARTIN 29-3-1997

Crusade

Welcome to the badlands
shake hands with your soul,
look back towards the future
noone understands.
Feeling lonely without you
turned away with love,
smiling eyes sent to help me
from the Heavens above.

Welcome to the badlands
this is where you belong,
looking forward to the past
hopeless longings so strong.
Only terror to guide you
forlorn feelings not meant to last,
hopeless thoughts to sustain you
now the Angels have past.

Temperature rising
as the light begins to fade,
the sound of Angels receding
as you drift through the shade.

Welcome to the badlands
approach my throne with fear,
leave the Angels behind you
wipe away those false tears.
Allow my strength to enfold you
to remove all the pain,
open your heart to my forgiveness
wallow in the glory of the one true name.

Welcome to the badlands
rejoice in this new life
glory in the power I place in your hands.
Release the pain and strife
you endured for so long,
cut loose the restraining bands
of such a worthless life,
use my love to make your heart strong.

Coming home at last
travel safe and swift
escape the past
accept my gift.

Welcome to the badlands
enjoy the fruit of battle,
glorious prizes for the winners,
shake the sun,moon and stars
cause the Heavens to rattle,
cover eternity with scars
parry the sword bravely,grasp the nettle,
no glory here for Gods sinners.

Welcome to the badlands
drowning in blood
crucify existence
hold the balance in your hands.
Trying to resist does no good
your life belongs to me for as long
as the wind shapes the sand
and the rain washes away the blood.

Kneel before me
bare your soul in my presence,
graduation is imminent
no more lessons.

Welcome to the badlands
serve me well to ensure your future,

heading towards armageddon
hoping to survive,
searching for salvation
amid a strange new culture,
death must be swift to achieve creation,
you must obeye your fears if you crave
salvation.

Return from the badlands
time to go home,grasp it firmly
now your life is in your hands.
Rivers of blood no more
save the joy of creation
rescue the relics of life
cause all to live as one nation.

TONY MARTIN 18-07-2011.

Dancing on the Sun

by Tony Martin on Nov 12, 2010.

Such a beautiful day
I feel like dancing on the sun
Feelings of happiness
A day full of fun.

Harmonious friendships
Lessons to be learned
Teachers asking questions
Merits to be earned.

Puzzles full of symbols
Numerical letters
Numbers made of shapes
Looks like a foriegn language
Then it all falls into place.

TONY MARTIN 13-11-2010

(my grandson,7,said he had good day at school, made him feel like dancing on the sun)

Dear Sister

It seems so long now since I came to you with my story,and I realise now after all the trouble and pain I caused you suffer on my behalf that you too have a life to live,but in times of strife and unknowing a man turns his soul to whoever he thinks will understand the melancholy which surrounds his entire being.
I feel a love for you now that I never thought possible from brother to sister.The crime I committed can never be forgiven,not even by GOD himself.What I did was totally selfish,a selfishness that was meant only to benefit me.How I could act that way I will never know.The only hope I have left is that someone will be able to explain why these things
happen.
You dear sister will always
remain for me the only friend I had in
times of need,everything I told you
was at the time exactly how I felt,
and the things I did at that time I
thought were necessary for me.
The reason I now languish in
this prison,the deed that brought me
here I also thought,in fact I knew to
be necessary at the time,AH but time
simply would not wait for me to decide.Now dear sister I have all the
time I ever wanted,but what good is
time to one such as I.
How does one such as
I spend time,time that will now turn
to eternity,money I can and have
spent,life I have spent although not
always wisely,sometimes disgracefully,
often with humour,and sometimes
with sorrow,friendships I have spent,
often wasted,but time I must now

spend alone in this cell.
Once again I ask of
you something I have no right to ask,
for what I did I know I must pay and
if necessary with my life,but for me
to pay this way seems to me to be
totally inhuman,for me to be left in
total isolation for eternity seems to be punishment beyond all human
endurance.I do not and will not ask
forgiveness for what I did,in this
life we all do wrong and we all suffer
wrong done to us,this is part of life,
some manage to cope,some suffer in
silence,others hit back,unfortunately
for me I chose the third option.
My request to you now
is that as you go through your life,
at the times you do wrong,as you will,
you will not allow yourself too much
self recrimination,and at the times when you are wronged you will not
allow the wrongdoers to punish
themselves,as I did for too long,you
must hit back with as much positive feeling for yourself as you can find in
your heart.Always look to yourself,for
one thing I have learned in my life is
that no matter who you are or how
many people you count as friends
when the time comes that you have
to account for the time you have
spent,then you will be alone for whatever time you have left.
This cell I now occupy
in my mind is so full and yet so empty
and time goes so slow.The part of my sentence which hurts the most is
that I am my own gaoler and I cannot
free myself,I cannot find the holder
of the key.
My final request is that you never desert me in your heart,
always think of me as your fool.
Goodbye dear sister,
Yours for all time.
Tony Martin 24-10-1993.

Depression

A feeling of blackness
forboding
filled,spilling over with gloom,
harshness
sharp as Sweeney Todd's razor,
blood red molten heat
painful
glowing bright as Satan's eyes
fearful to behold
filling my world with doom.

Forcing the breath inside to burn
through the walls of life,
boiling through my veins
towards the temple which
sustains me through these times of strife,
forcing a path towards my brain
pausing only to torture my soul,
where are you?

Each time the feeling goes deeper
destroying the thoughts
and feelings of tenderness and loving caresses
joys of serenity gone,
deeper still,
the heat inside grows until all I see
are the thoughts of Satan
glowing in those burning eyes.

Feeding,bleeding,creeping
the pain entering my mind,

colours collide bouncing furiously
from one thought to another,
images of good and evil
swim alongside each other
until?
once again the heat subsides.

Blood red softens into watery pink
as the evil begins to sink
vowing to return once again
to creat more turmoil and strife
fighting the goodness inside,
a battle constructed by this feeling
of not knowing how best to live this life.

Conflicting loyalties between jealousy and love
each trying to turn the tide
attempting to kill off the fortitude
of this once glowing light
that shone through the gloom
and radiated towards a once glowing heart.

These battles now more frequent and bitter
how many more will I have to fight?
can the strength within sustain my love for life
or will the glowing heat of this depression
finally take it's toll
and destroy this spirit
within my soul.

Craving the answer is part of the problem
and feeds the enemy within,
if only I could live without
this need for answers
then maybe I could join hands
with the happy dancers.

TONY MARTIN 11-6-2011

Dog Collar Hatred

by Tony Martin on Nov 17, 2010.

At the end of the day
Just before the light fades away
People will moan
This tired old world will groan.

Is it really peace we crave
How many should we save
The hatred is now fading
Put the guns in their own grave.

Talking is easy cheaper and safe
But will it achieve the happiness sought
Or will the guns reappear
The battles once more to be fought.

So many lives given,taken in sin
Yet the collar still shines
Which side will win
Old ideas in a new constitution.

Forceful hatred for so many years
Flashes of light explosions to be heard
Pain mutilation and tears
Instead of a peaceful word.

Join hands now never let go
Retaliate with love
Let happiness show
Try on the other glove.

Let the children see what it was like before
Show them a life without war
Teach them to smile
Let the mourning cease
Give them a life full of happiness
And peace.

LET THEM HAVE THEIR SAY
BEFORE THE LIGHT FADES AWAY.

TONY MARTIN 17-11-2010

Dreamcatcher

by Tony Martin on Apr 3.

Steel grey eyes
cloud covered full moon
drifting slowly through the gloom,
snow covered pine
chilly winters night
echoes of your mournful whine
causing sensations of eerie fright.
Dreamcatcher padding softly through the moonlit mist
searching hungrily
for the demons the night has kissed.
Soft luxuriant fur glistening
with early morning dew
silent as the star kissed ghost of the sacred christening,
ancient as time itself.
Dreamcatcher welcome
enter my night,
softly grasp these thoughts that occupy my mind in this lonely time,
ease into the dawn
bring me safely home.
'Tis now time to awaken
leaving behind the ghosts of the night,
lower me softly through the clouds of dreams
that disturb the peace of my night,
Dreamcatcher before you go
reassure me that when needed
your steely grey eyes will once again glow.

TONY MARTIN. 2-4-2011

Empty Corners

Empty corners with spaces in between
All this room,what does it mean.
Passing slowly through these spaces
Below the surface
Under the ceiling of this lonely room.
Through the darkness she came
Drawing light from beyond the grave
Leaving behind all the pain.
Death follows slowly
Bringing life to us all
A life to be savoured,used to create
Until she beckons once more.
The magic has gone along with the hurt
All that is left now
Is the pain and the dirt.

TONY MARTIN 13-11-2010.

Empty Promises

by Tony Martin on Feb 16, 2010. © TONY MARTIN, All rights reserved

Empty promises
from an empty mind
trails of honesty
difficult to find
Empty heart
in a world of deceit
empty eyes of people
yet to meet
Empty soul
devoid of love
empty promises
scattered from above
Empty aura
surrounding us all
empty world destined to fall
Empty spirit
inside you and me
EMPTY PROMISE
to set me free

Flaming Teardrops

Btween the wrinkles of
Another wasted night
Lie the troubled thoughts
Of a man in fright.

Tonight I may succumb
To the pressures of life
I have even thought
About the love I once felt for my wife.

Why is it such a waste
To remember the past
Are the good times
Never meant to last.

The tears sometimes still flow
Each teardrop so full
With the warmth
From the candle which was meant to glow.

Flaming teardrops
Light up the darkness of life
Recreating the love
I still feel for my wife.

Tony Martin 25-11-1996

for Pauline

by Tony Martin on Dec 12, 2010. © TONY MARTIN,

Where is my star
Where are you tonight
Remove from me these clouds
Which cover my sight.
Let me see you again
Let me live in your glow
Remove from me this pain
Which continues to grow.
Once again
Shine through the night
Watch over me
Ease this feeling of fright.
Allow me your prescence
Take my soul to your heart
Ease the doubts
Which I sense are keeping us apart.

Tony Martin 20-10-1996

for the Love of a Bruise

Just another statistic
A number
Black on white
Does this make life more realistic
What a terrible sight.

You have become a shadow
Such a waste of grace
I dread tomorrow
I no longer want to see your face.

Such poise you once possessed
Peace and serenity was yours
Only I ever guessed
You preferred to fight wars.

Tony Martin 1-2-1997

Forgotten Memory

by Tony Martin on Mar 15, 2010. © TONY MARTIN, All rights reserved

You have taken the place
Of my memory,
Removed from the future
What used to be,
It's all gone to far
There is no going back
BUT
How long can I wait for you to say yes to me.

TONY MARTIN

Forgotten Story

Below the height of sensibility
Nothing stirs
To move would create a disturbance
So catastrophic the Prince of evil
Could never concieve.

There is a stillness in the air
A sensation of death which I fear
But wait
Young wind stir this life
Remove from it the turmoil and guilt
Refresh what is left
Cover whatever we spilled.

Falling leaves flutter in the damp air
Settling softly through the mist
Is it fear
Or are we just afraid of the twist
In the story which is about to appear.

Slowly 'tis emerging through the thoughts of days gone by
Trying to forget is not easy
Would it help to cry.

Carry it softly
Ease the pain from your soul
Help me to deliver
We all crave the same goal
Settle softly into the memories of what used to be
Allow the restlessness to fade
If all are not to see.

The feeling of serenity now takes over
Yet this story I still wish to uncover.

I will help you
If you promise not to hurt me
What I did was unforgiveable
But I had no choice.

I don't know if I can allow you to tell your part
Will you tell it your way
Or will you allow it to come from the heart.
Whichever way this story is told we will never agree
Neither of us wishes to take the blame
For dowsing such a bright flame.

Why did you allow me to do it
How could I have been so naive
What was it you wanted
I really did believe.

We should have helped each other
But our directions wavered
To be part of your life forever
Was all I ever desired.

How can you say these things
Why do you lie with your eyes
I could never understand why it was I you had to despise,
The hate I now feel for you is so wrong
But how can I stop it
I have never been that strong.

You threw me away
Destroyed what I offered
So now here we are,left with the gift of life
Yet so alone without the love which was offered.

Just a whisper
A pretended kiss

What would have happened
If my cheek you had missed.
They all thought you loved me
Just the same as them
Such is the frailty of men.
Too late now even for me to forgive
For destroying the life we desired
You cannot be allowed to live.

Must I spin this coin again
It stil has only two sides
Each time you win the toss
Causes me so much pain
But this feeling I must hide.
No places left now to conceal my pain
Believe me I have tried
Yet through all my suffering
There simply has been no gain.

'Tis time for me to retaliate
Against those who repaid me with scorn
How many times can a cheek be turned
If I return once more will you listen
How many times can a cross be burned
My cheeks with your tears still glisten.
How many times will the truth be spurned
Next time will you listen
Why must my decisions always be overturned
These tears on my cheeks still glisten.

I will try to answer I will do my best
What really happened I am not sure
But I think I failed the test
You were never easy to understand
You expected too much dedication
What was I supposed to do
I needed a different sensation.
The love you asked for I didn't have
Even my life was not mine to give
Yet still you demanded

Quietely it seems
But the pressure was still there
Even in my dreams.

Would you have done the same
How would you have reacted
If yours had been
MY NAME.

TONY MARTIN 15-6-1995.

Fragrance of the Night

by Tony Martin on Feb 1. © TONY MARTIN,

The fragrance of the night
Soft and warm
To be inhaled on sight
So soothing to the mind
Keeps the body calm.
To float on this aroma
To sail on the breeze
Which brings relief from the coma
Of futures disease.
Patience is given
Relaxation takes over
Calmness
Frantic life taken from a generous lover.
Through the clouds drifting this way
Just one more deep breath
Will take the torture away,
Clear the smoke,help me to see
Is this some kind of joke
Am I the fool we all would like to be.
Come down slowly
Allow your mind to relax
Ease your body through the gift of forgiveness
The only commodity for which
There is no tax.

TONY MARTIN 14-11-1996

Fresh Kindling

Rake out the ashes
leave nothing behind,
clean out the hearth
draw the debris from your mind,
gather fresh kindling
capture the feelings
drifting in on the wind,
floating by on gossamer wings
energy for the soul,
enticing angels to sing
a serenade to strengthen your heart.

TONY MARTIN 22-4-2011

From Boy to Man

Tonight it begins
the end,
shuddering excitement
eclipsing the innocence
of radiant desire,
the desire of lustful romance.
the end
of the wasteful anticipation
of youthful exuberance,
paralized with anticipation,
spread eagled
across the softly growing comforts of life.
the end
of frustrating limitations
which dwell in the mind,
flowing freely now
leaving adolesence behind,
the joy of discovery
excitement to share
inhibitions discarded
beneath the moon's watchful stare,
softness and warmth through each caress,
resistance relinquished
along with your dress,
searching for fulfillment
pleasure to give,
slowly exploring,
senses aflame,
joining together,
breathing your name.
thunderous feelings,explosions of lust

holding on to each other
sharing love's secret trust.
eruptions of joy releasing me as only you can
only you had the power
to turn that boy into this man.

TONY MARTIN 10-03-2011

From the Grave
(Vengeance is Mine Sayeth the Lord)

by Tony Martin on Feb 1. © TONY MARTIN, All rights reserved

Twist the rope
Help the knot to form
Slowly apply the pressure
Make them regret being born.

Remove from them
That which they steal from others
Force them to realise
What it feels like to be mothers.

Death for them was easy to give
BUT
If I can't share your world
Then why should they live.

All they had to do was ask
If my breath they wanted to share
For me that would be an easy task
BUT
They just didn't care.

TONY MARTIN 11-2-1997

Future History

As the outer rim of the circle becomes broken
And the light shines through
A multitude of sins become apparent
As this light becomes brighter,stronger,yet softer
The sins of the forefathers become easier to understand
Great strength is taken from the comfort that is offered
Understanding is given to those willing to learn.

So many years ago
Seems like only yesterday
Will we pay forever or will it all end today
Reminders of memories best forgotten
Or is it wiser to show new minds what occurred
Should they witness the tragedies created by the greed of those without need
Can they see past the rim of the circle of bright light
Will they grasp the strength offered
Are they prepared to learn from the comfort of understanding
Only then will the reminders of such memories
Prevent further tragedies.

Are these new minds strong enough
To accept the responsibility for the future of mankind
Are they capable of laying these memories to rest
Will these sins eventually be forgiven
So mankind can live in peace
I think not
Or are these memories to be repeated
I think so
'TIS ALL HISTORY BEING BORN.

TONY MARTIN.

Get Well Soon

Draw strength
From all who surround you
Use their love
Some of which may astound you.

Help yourself
To the warmth that they offer
Allow your resistance to acceptance
To grow softer.

Tony Martin 18-10-1996

God's Gift

by Tony Martin on Dec 22, 2010. © TONY MARTIN, All rights reserved

Reflections of life
Mirrored through love
In crystal clear waters
Sent from above.

Surrounded by strength
Keeping darkness at bay
Holding evil at arms length
Bringing hope for a new day.

God's creation
Offered generously to man
Joyous salvation
As only HE can.

GUESS WHO

Guess who looks after the night
Who waits patiently for the light.

Guess who looks after the dawn
Waiting for the air to turn warm.

Guess who is watching when you fail to wake
Waiting for you to make a mistake.

Guess who follows when you surface confused
Gathering the remnants of dreams you used.

Guess who cleanses the doubts you feel
After you realise the fear was unreal.

Guess who returns to help you recover
After confusion with a jealous lover.

Guess who holds your hand each time the tears flow
Offering the love only He can show.

Guess who surrounds you with love from dusk 'til dawn
Protecting you from a crown of thorns.

Guess why you cannot feel
The love you are offered is oh so real.

The answers you seek dwell in the stars above
Protecting your life with celestial love.

TONY MARTIN. 25-08-2011.

GUILT

by Tony Martin on Jul 26. © TONY MARTIN, All rights reserved

You cannot hide within me,
now is the time to learn
the truth is never free,
and freedom from guilt you must earn.
To be released and for given
to set your spirit free
the past from the future must be driven
and the soul allowed to see.
When wrongs are admitted
and the guilt has been swallowed,
when the silence has been lifted
only then is redemption allowed.
The guilty die
hopefully in pain,
after a lifetime living a lie
still noone knows your name.
TONY MARTIN 22-07-2011

Hiding In the Mist

How long must we remain
Hidden from view
Sharing the pain
Which passes slowly from me to you.

Hiding in the mist
Surrounded by love
Just hoping to be kissed
With blessings from above.

The warmth you release
Glowing in the dark
Fills me with peace
As well as a spark.

Shrouded in mist
Drowning in love
Still hoping to be kissed
With blessings from above.

Swirling through the mist
Gathering Angels surrounded by love
Shall this be the moment we are kissed
With blessings from above.

TONY MARTIN 23-11-2010.

43

I Think I Know

I know what it is
I know why it's there
I even know what's caused it
Too much beer.

So,cut it out
Remove it from your life
Don't leave this one
As long as you did your wife.

There are things which occur
Things we don't plan
Some of them just happen
I hope I can cope,do YOU think I can.

It used to be easy
Life was so much fun
Then we grew up
That's when the heartaches begun.

Tony Martin 21-1-1997

If You Love Me

If you love me
leave me alone
allow me to drown my sorrows in your tears,
allow your leaving to bring me peace
even through your fears.

If you love me
do not mourn
the passing of love's tenderness
but rejoice in this new creation
of life's forgetfulness.

If you love me
please walk away
don't look over your shoulder
on this dreadful day.

If you love me
now my life is over
the forgiveness is yours
to share with a generous lover.

If you love me
after the pain I created
then my new journey
will be easier
knowing you would have waited.

If you love me
after the noose tightens
then walk away proudly
and know that I love you
and sing your name loudly.

TONY MARTIN 26-06-2011

In Dreams

by Tony Martin on Mar 21. © TONY MARTIN,

Encased in the love
of each other's charms,
encircled by the warmth
of two loving arms.
Only in dreams now do you appear
easing the loneliness
of each tragic tear,
drifting towards twilight
through the pleasures of loves dream
not really knowing
of what should have been.
When the flame of love
was still glowing
a love stolen,
taken away
destroyed by a lie
a mind driven by envy.
Tears form once again
as memories through dreams
return me to a time
when the joy of love
didn't seem to be a crime.
And now through each waking hour
when I see you pass by
adolesence returns
reminding me of a time
before tears filled the sky.

TONY MARTIN 21-3-2011.

Just a Couple of Thoughts

The tragedy of adolescent naivety
Created by teenage exuberance
Whilst learning of life
Through the heartache of puberty.

Every fear hides a wish
Every promise hides a lie
The only comfort we recieve is when we die.

STRANGE LIFE

What a strange life I do live
Wanting everything
Nothing to give
What a strange way I do look at love
Wanting everything
Especially from above
What a strange feeling this lust for life
Just as strong now
As when you were my wife.

MY PRAYER

So now I lay down and dream of you
At the end of this lonely night what else can I do
Except reach out for tomorrow
Using ideas you allow me to borrow.

TONY MARTIN 30-9-2005

Just for Me

What is it that moves
Beneath the timbers of life,
As the distant past
Comes rushing through the corridors of my memory,
Pictures of a life,
Visions of wonders yet to come,
Passing slowly through my mind
As fresh air through the open windows
Of this lonely room.

LAUGHTER IN THE DARK

Deep into the shadows
As the light disappears
Drifting through the hollows
Trembling with fear
All the loneliness and despair
Slowly follow.
Sinking softly into oblivion
Through the creation of dreams
Once again proving
This life is not how it seems.

Foetal beneath the covers
Drifting through nervous clouds
Searching for forgotten lovers
Through misty damp shrouds.
Opening the mind,
Losing all reality,
Thoughts drifting on the wind
Through love's gracious insanity.

Returning through the void
Into the beauty of rebirth
Leaving behind the pain and trauma
Returning to mother earth.
Throwing back the covers
To be born again
Forcing loose the grip held by past lovers
Waking to the joys of a new refrain.

Laughter in the dark
Is all that remains
Of a long ago time
When we all had sweeter names.

TONY MARTIN. 24-08 2011.

Life or Death

To die as I live
I must be alone
There is no more to give
No fear to be shown.

I know where I am going
I remember so well
Why should I not
This place seems like hell.

A world with no sorrow
Just happiness abounds
No tears to be heard
Just pleasant sounds.

To live through death
Is such a travesty
Yet to die without life
Shall this be my destiny.

TONY MARTIN 22-11—2010

LIMP FLAGS (*Europe*)

by Tony Martin on Feb 1. © TONY MARTIN, All rights reserved

Still the dampness descends
Creating lucid visions
Of forgetfullness,
How long will it last
Must we fight again,
This time around noone will know
Or remember the past.

Bullet proof
Immune to the pain
Can you see my face,if so
Then feel my shame.

Feel the pain that I see
Take your guidance from me
Help yourself to my strength
Make one last effort
Seek my guidance at length,
The freedom and peace that I crave
Sadly,this has cost us dearly
Filled more than one grave.

To create one union
To sew these limp flags together
Is this really the solution
Or are we better to disagree forever.

TONY MARTIN 6-3-1997

Long Into the Night, for Pauline.

by Tony Martin on Dec 12, 2010.

Once I wrote a poem
Twice I wrote a song
Still I remain alone
The words did not belong.

The music is there
All the notes rhyme
Will the doubts ever clear
Will she never be mine.

This song that I sing
These poems I write
I still hear the bells ring
Long into the night.

It's time for bed
Time to lie down
Help me to discover
If I still wear the crown.

Tony Martin 21-1-1997.

Lucky Me

by Tony Martin on Feb 1. © TONY MARTIN, All rights reserved

How lucky I have been
To have witnessed the things I have seen
Such joys and sorrow
Beauty and tenderness
These things
Was I only meant to borrow.
From whence these things came
I now return them
Only joyful memories remain
And only time can destroy them,
Through my life they passed
Just like shifting sand
Was there something elsc for which I should have asked
Or have you given all you have for mortal man.

TONY MARTIN 30-8-1996

My Life, P.S.

by Tony Martin on Mar 15, 2010. © TONY MARTIN, All rights reserved

Why have I created this monster inside of me
When will I allow my soul to be free
To roam through the night
Living the life I deserve

Once more to smile
To forget this feeling of hatred
Once again to give love
Feeling as one with this life I am offered

Will I ever forgive the indiscretions of matrimony
Situations which destoyed a life so full of hope
Promises I made just to myself
Dreams of contentment just to be left on the shelf

Such a crowded place this precarious ledge
Just one final push and
I am over the edge

SO, Will I ever know why
I created this life
Would it all have been different
Had you been my wife.

TONY MARTIN

My Own Kind

by Tony Martin on Dec 31, 2010. © TONY MARTIN,

Aimlessly drifting on the
Highways of life,
Following the contours of a
Twisted mind,
The curve I now negotiate
Is so filled with strife
How long must I search
To find my own kind.

Travelling now in a straight line
No twists or turns to follow,
Sometimes too fast
Other times having the truth to swallow.

Being made to wait
For the life I was promised
Having destroyed with help
The one I was given,
We are all Gods born of lesser men
Waiting for the time
Which will make this life worth living.

TONY MARTIN 27-7-1997

My Sons

You are the sons of a man
With a troubled mind
Take care of yourselves
And my grandchildren
Leave the past behind.

Too many stories to be told
Some may not seem true,
The past is all mine
The future is for you.

Help yourselves to what remains
Seek neither mercy or forgiveness,
Never trust to Ladyluck
For she will always leave you thirsty.

Tony Martin 21-10-1996.

Mystical Hindsight

The teardrops on mycheeks wil soon fade away
Leaving hope for me
Of a life from yesterday
Happiness and fun
Tenderness and beauty
A lust for life second to none.

Second time around love's not gone.

I sat in the dark tonight
Contemplating the wrong and the right
Thinking of friends and times gone by
Then you came to light explaining the truth
Which I thought could not be right.

Second time around life's just as good.

Nail me to the sky
Watch the clouds form a cross as my life passes by
Annoint your soul with my teardrops
Drink my blood as you witness me die
Embrace my thoughts as you walk away
Carry my soul
Keep me with you until your dying day.

First time around death holds no fear.

Through the power of mystical hindsight
Treat yourself to the realities of life
Only then will you know the true meaning of love.

Second time around love's not gone.

No Direction Home

Will this road never end?
If only this was the final bend,
Again the mist is falling
Blurring the hoped for vision,
The sight which would end
All this indecision.
The beginning of a glow
Just around the next curve,
Will you be able to hold it?
Your fragile nerve.
Fading once again
As the bend is left behind,
Stretching out before you
Or is it all in your mind?
Carry on,continue to try
Noone must see you crying,
BUT,
Even after all these wasted tears
Never stop trying.
Destination approaches,
Solitude encroaches,
Companions on this journey are few
Friends left behind are many,
These solitary steps were meant just for you.
Another bend comes into view
Glowing brighter than the last,
Steps quicken,breathing heavy now
Heart beating fast.
Dispelling the fear of pursuing dread
Controlling the pain
Inside your head,

Fading again
Steps retreating into the gloom,
Disappearing behind the walls
Of this dreary tomb.
Darkness returns
Burying the glow of life,
Is this the place
of which you wanted
The secrets to be shown?
The place from where there is
NO DIRECTION HOME.

TONY MARTIN 5-03-2011.

No

No commandments to live by?
No,more terror.
No sins of the fathers to hide from?
No,more fear.
No fogiveness even from the one betrayed?
No,more dying.
No hatred especially for the dead?
No,more crying.
No more love not even from above?
No,more hunger.
No expectations to live up to?
No,more trying.
No suffering a future full of peace?
No,more lying.
No more searching for perfection?
No,easy selection.
No more visions of confusion?
No,more seclusion.
No more wondering what tomorrow may bring?
No,just accept anything.

TONY MARTIN 8-2-2011

One Last Inspection

by Tony Martin on Mar 8, 2010.

So dark and dusty
Silence now prevails
Such a long way to go
Just follow the rails.

No light to be seen
Not a sound to be heard
Just a feeling of emptiness
There is no other word.

Not much further now
Steps quickened with fear
Soon be all over
Seems the end is so near.

Fooled by the silence
Reality distorted by the dark
This sensation of loneliness
Makes a soul shiver as blown leaves in the park.

Footsteps and groaning
Imagination running wild
Creaking timbers,whistling wind
Undreampt of dangers make the blood run cold.

Seems like a lifetime
This time around.
The sound of men working
Now gone from underground.

All that is left now

Is a dark dusty hole
Soon to be covered
No more use now for our coal.

One last inspection
Memories never forgotten
These feelings make me realise
This whole world is turning rotten.

TONY MARTIN 09-03-2010

Out of Anger

by Tony Martin on Jun 5.

Out of anger comes
honesty and love
emotions of turmoil
hand in glove.
Quelling feelings
of unrighteous glory
brought forth with
the determination
to relate the story
of a lifetime of recrimination
and torture suffered
because of lies and sensation
for thrills of illicit enjoyment
delivered with tenderness and a smile.
Emotional blackmail fired through
sparkling eyes into the void
of a once loving heart
which was broken but still lives
with the hope of a return to the days
that became a highway into the abyss
that was the world of lonely wives.

TONY MARTIN 4-06-2011.

Out of the Darkness

Out of the darkness
forcing aside the brightness of life,
consuming all the love and happiness
burning feelings,
creating strife.
Glowing with the anger of consumate hatred,
hatred for all of creations beauty,
Surrounded by a darkness
the depth of which cannot be measured,
Dreamlike,
Nightmarish,
Closing in,
drawing strength from the fear that precedes
the advancing force of hatred.
Darkness growing stronger
contemplating the victory craved for so long.
at last the power of evil will sustain the truth,
the truth hidden by dreams of bright glowing embers,
embers of feelings for the acceptance of promises,
promises of a salvation belonging to forgotten dreams.
Dreams and promises,
leftovers from the death of hope,
Sacrifice,
No more too give,
Safe,
within the warmth of the beauty of creation,
fighting to live,
just one last time force the darkness away
increase the strength of your light,
create a new day.
Return,

bring new life through the turmoil of darkness,
share the warmth from the glow of your crown
easing back the hatred of that long black gown.
Following your footsteps
embraced by your love,
once again safe
in the glow from above.

TONY MARTIN 2-5-2011.

Pains Clay

by Tony Martin on Jun 27. © TONY MARTIN, All rights reserved

Lovingly from pains clay
mould this moment with creativity,
sensually sculpt with ingenuity
the free flowing eternal spring,
ever caressing your subconcious desire
with the fluidity
that your fingertips bring.

TONY MARTIN 26-06-2011

Peaceful Waters

The stillness of the night
Replaces nothing for me
Yet,shall the daylight
Return you from the sea.

Peaceful serenity abounds,
Your ship floating gently
Through the darkness
Without sound.

Still waters at night
Are the visions I see,
Yet through the daylight
These thoughts do trouble me.

Flashes of light
Came from the Sun,I thought,
Little did I know
Against these demons you fought.

To be alone against these dangers
While I remain here
Wallowing in my own fear
Driven by loneliness and selfish tears.

Flashes of light once more from the sun
I thought,
Cannon fire,explosions from above,
Still you will return from the sea
Once more to accept my love.

Tony Martin

When the wind rises as darkness falls
Serene contentment replaces these walls,
Do you feel it too?
Cannon fire,flashes of light
Explosions from me to you.

The loneliness I fear do you feel it too,
Through the dark hours what do you see,
Through the flashes of light
Do you see me.?

Yes I do see you through the flashes of light
Yet my mind is filled with terrible fright,
All through the dark hours they come
These explosions from above
From you to me you said with love.

I see you more clearly
Now the battering eases
Cannon fire,flashes of light are not from above
So the worrying increases.

Now I feel death all around me
As the cold enters the fray
Snow ice and frost
Please help me to pray.

Now the loneliness creaps over me
As I float through these waves
Will I survive to return
From this watery grave?

All is lost everyone else is gone
And now I am sinking,no longer alone,
Through the darkness I see what it is that awaits me
So much peace and understanding,at last I shall rest
To be where I belong,
I know I will miss you, will you follow me soon?
I cannot return for this is MY walk on the moon.

The pain is now gone but the longing remains
So many good men who will remember thier names,?
Surrounded by water
Covered with foam
How long must we wait until they bring us home?

Will you still be there where I saw you last
Or am I just a memory now from your troubled past?

Ice closes in
Covering and cleansing with strength,
Is it worth it,will the fighting never cease?
Close to the bottom now,soon be at rest
Sorry we lost but we gave our best,
Settling now so far from the surface
All the pain is now gone
Cannon fire,flashes of light
Explosions from the Sun.

TONY MARTIN 21-6-1995.

Pure Fantasy

The joy of a pure thought
Causing sensations you never knew existed
A spine chilling caress
Holding life in it's mercy
Gently lifting
Carrying you away on the cloud of a fantasy
Bringing joy to each new day
Brightly glowing stars drifting slowly through your mind
Opening up your heart
To a new love floating on the wind
Hold on to this one
Do not let it slip
Gently caress the love you desire
Open up your soul
Feel the warmth of love's fire.

Saving Grace

Will you accept what I have to give
Will you allow me my life to live
Take what I have there is no more to offer
Leave nothing for me allow me to suffer
The hours I have spent in this dark dreary place
I think
Are enough for me to recover with
THE SAVING GRACE.

Say Goodbye

Please,take her away
Allow me to live
There is no more I can say
I have no more to give.

At last
'Tis time to say goodbye
Just close the door
I won't cry.

The love that I feel
Will outlive this pain
No hatred to conceal
Just the future to gain.

Take care of yourself
Leave others to worry
Only hatred is concieved
By asking the soul to hurry.

Tony Martin 5-2-1997

Shadow of Life

Crawling through the mist
gasping for breath,
from the depth of the darkness
came the shadow of life,
struggling to sustain
the slender hold
on the pleasure of this pain,
slipping into the world
once left behind
searching for fulfillment
through a devious mind,
climbing back from oblivion
through the haze,
calling out through the silence
seeking help to survive
not wishing to remain in this lonely hell,
drifting back into the fire
through the thickening mist
weakening senses unable to resist,
back into the darkness through the shadow of life
ever deeper,
slowly sinking,
burning fever
going now,sinking fast.
colliding with oblivion
rushing madly towards the past,
BANG,
God the pain as release holds my hand
painful needles on returning
from hell's forbidden land,
burning flesh soaked with sweat,

brain frantically searching for an answer
to this fearful threat,
waking slowly,
eyes streaming with tears
no more sorrow now for me
after crushing these fears,
shaking,
happiness abounds
covered with glory and welcoming sounds,
"success" they say,
"welcome back,"
but once they're all gone leaving me to contemplate
will I once again seek HELL
the mist which I know is my fate.

TONY MARTIN 9-03-2011.

Shallow Contempt

by Tony Martin on Aug 5. © TONY MARTIN, All rights reserved

I see you inside me
but I will not follow,
the sadness you cause
leaves me feeling so shallow,
the path I chose
could be long and arduous
but to follow you
would be too dangerous.
Life for me has never been easy,
I blamed you for that,
but the choices were mine to make,
did I make the wrong one
while feeling contemptuous.

TONY MARTIN 27-7-2011

Sleepless Nights

I should go to sleep but if I do
Who knows I may never wake.

If I do go to sleep and can't return
Will you come to get me
And keep me from harm.
This place where I sleep
Is so empty it scares me,
It's so cold and lonely
When you're not near me,
I used to hold you
Not always so tight,
Just to be near you
Helped me through the night.
To know I am lonely
Gives me such a fright,
And the worst time of all
Is all through the night,
Sometimes when I sleep
I dream you are here
It seems so real
To feel you so near.
Then I awaken
And you are gone
Your heart has been taken
By another one,
If only your body
Was once again near me
To hold and to love you
Would once again cheer me.
Your love so warm

Eyes that caught fire
My love for you will go on
And never tire,
I feel so tired I will have to sleep
If I don't wake
My love you can keep.

TONY MARTIN 1993.
son of man.

GUILT

by Tony Martin on Jul 26. © TONY MARTIN, All rights reserved

You cannot hide within me,
now is the time to learn
the truth is never free,
and freedom from guilt you must earn.
To be released and forgiven
to set your spirit free
the past from the future must be driven
and the soul allowed to see.
When wrongs are admitted
and the guilt has been swallowed,
when the silence has been lifted
only then is redemption allowed.
The guilty die
hopefully in pain,
after a lifetime living a lie
still noone knows your name.
TONY MARTIN 22-07-2011

Spider's Lament

Spider in the sink,
Is he looking for a drink?
Turn on the tap,watch him run
Trying to reach the rim
MY GOD,
Doesn't he know how to swim.

The water's rising,
Can't climb any higher.
MY GOD
This is worse than running away from fire.

Nearly made it
Just one more step,
Can't afford another slip
Already to wet.

Turn off the tap
Watch the water subside
Spider breathes easy,
MY GOD
Just likeold Canute
When he sat watching the tide.

Nothing changes
Insect or man.
MY GOD
Why do we all imagine we can do
What only you can.

TONY MARTIN

Spirits of the Night

As the darkness falls
and silence covers the room
the spirits of the night fill my heart with gloom,
sadness prevails
so heavy is this feeling of doom,
forgiveness nowhere to be found
in the sadness of this lonely room.
The darkness grows deeper,
no more sound,
crushing my soul
with the power of life's eternal keeper.
Pressure increases as tears begin to fall
the saltiness of dread trickles across my lips
as the weight of the night
held in the grasp of these deadly spirits delivers
it's final fright,
what is left as death takes over?
as life drifts away
from below the night time spirit's cover.
The saltiness increases
as the tears of fright burn their way towards my aching heart,
leaving a trail of desperation
as the darkness grows deeper
causing a deathly sensation
within this frightened sleeper.
Will the light of the dawn reappear
driving out the spirits of the night
banishing them with the sensation of fear
that surrounds life's glowing light,
bringing forth a new day
to dilute the saltiness of each deathly tear.

Spirits of the night be gone,
once again drowned by the light of day,
the tears now dry,
saltiness sweetened by the joys of life
relieving the depression of the night's dark strife.

TONY MARTIN. 2-4-2011

Stillness

It only moved a fraction
Less than the breadth of a breeze
To grasp it would have been foolish
Even a gentle squeeze.

Yet,something stirred in the shiver
Reflecting light which didn't exist,
Something moving through the light of a shimmer
In the stillness of the mist.

Death never comes easy,some call it peace
Glides in without warning
On the breath of a breeze
Stirring memories of a lifetime now lost in the mist
Leaving hope for a love shattered by a kiss.

Breakable futures lingered
Through the darkness of despair,
Carrying love through the mist of a lifetime
Fragile as a crystal chandelier.

Sparkling in the sunlight
Reflecting love blowing in with the breeze,
Let it pass this time,let the breeze shimmer through
Let the warmth of the Angels caress you,
Kiss their wings as the night watches you.

When this dream is over,when the breeze turns to storm,
When the light disappears into darkness
And the shimmer dies in the mist
Open your arms for the Angels,accept their welcoming kiss.

TONY MARTIN 11-02-2010

Talking Smoke

by Tony Martin on Mar 8, 2010. © TONY MARTIN,

Lets sit together on the floor
Smoke a pipe,talk some more
Listen to what I have to say
Bring tomorrow back from yesterday.

Surely it's not worth all this fuss
After all the discoveries are still with us
Can tomorrows people use them?
Of course we can,you are not the final man.

Then sit with me now on the floor
Smoke a pipe talk some more
I will listen to what you have to say
And send tomorrow back from yesterday.

It is so easy to learn
Yesterdays discoveries still grow
But will you listen to what I know?
If not then my knowledge you will have to earn.

So sit with me once more
Smoke a pipe talk some more
Let's all listen to what they said
Rescue tomorrow from yesterdays dead.

TONY MARTIN 09-03-2010

Tell Me It's Raining

I thought that it was raining
But now I see they are teardrops
I can't believe I am really crying
Will the heartaches never stop.

Pass along slowly
PLEASE
Move further down the line
Don't allow your heart to settle
'Til your mind is one with mine.

'Tis now time to invent
But not to grow old
If I can't have the life that was meant
Then I will have to settle
For the one you have sold.

Pass along slowly
PLEASE
Move further down the line
Has your heart settled
Or is it still mine.

Tony Martin 5-2-1997

the Assassins Reply

by Tony Martin on Nov 16, 2010. © TONY MARTIN, All rights reserved

The ability I have to create
is something that never fails
to amaze me,
although the only creation I am capable of
is DEATH.
Noone else views what I do as creation,
Destruction would be the description most
would apply to what I consider to be an
ART FORM.
Whatever you or I wish to call
this happening doesn't really matter
because as did PICASSO,MICHEALANGELO,or DA VINCI
Ialso derive great pleasure from my art.
Also the greater the passion at the time of
CREATION
The greater the pleasure after.

the Changing of the Tide

It wasn't very loud
The rattle of the chain
But each time you heard it
It seemed to call your name,
One to each corner
Of the cold marble slab.
As the picture formed
In side your mind
Causing nipples to become erect
Not knowing what to expect,
Behind the blindfold you could never be sure
Whether your tormentors numbered 3 or 4
Two hands across your breasts, one teasing your moistening lips
Who do they belong to,will you ever know
BUT,all that matters now is the tingling afterglow
Flowing freely now as two fingers find your centre,
RELAX was whispered as you strained against the chains,
What is that being foced into your mouth to prevent the scream
Of ecstasy from within,passion mounting quickly as the fingers are replaced
All control is lost as the table starts to turn,how many are there watching
As you are passed around,hands caressing everywhere,nipple clamps applied
Lips and tongues caress your body drinking of it's wine
The sensuous scream of ecstasy released as your mouth is opened wide
EMPTIED.as the table stops revolving and the ecstasy subsides you feel
Your life returning like the changing of the tides.

the Creaking Door

The creaking door,
The squeal of the hinges,
Open it slowly
Crawl through the gap,
Allow life to drift across the floor
How far to the other side,can you reach it.
Do you know if he is watching
Can he touch you,
Does your soul twist away
When he sees how you feel,
Will you ask him to stay.
One day drifts to the next
Night intervenes,creeps inbetween
Hiding the ghosts
That noone else has ever seen,
Sweat crawling through the holes in your skin,
What does it cost
How much life must you pay
Will your life be the same
When you send him away.

TONY MARTIN 09-01-2011

THE CUPBOARD (*under the stairs*)

Someone is in there
the cupboard under the stairs,
looking for a way out,but,
nobody cares.
Darkness and cold,unable to shout
fists clenched through fear,nerves on edge,
stairs creaking above
under the weight of each step
as heavy feet rise above each ledge,
is he going up,or coming down?
difficult to tell.
Further into the corner,darker there,
heartbeat quickens
holding back a tear,
Waiting for the handle to turn,
silence prevails as the air grows thicker
sweat oozing now
makes the skin feel slicker.
The handle turns slowly
then the rattle of the key,
the air pressure changes as the door begins to move,
hands tight together
a prayer offered up above.
Light slowly enters as the hinges groan loudly,
the mind gripped with fear,no place to hide
the corner grows smaller,skin begins to creep,
the door moving quicker now,hands reaching inside
approaching the corner
where it should have been safe to hide.
Is the door wide enough to run?
too late,

"gotcha"he growls,"now this is your fate"
strong hands grasping tight
squeezing harder,cutting off air,
keep fighting,push him away,
this is not fair.
Strength returning,fear drifting away,
one final push,show you still care
life is yours to keep don't just give it away.
Fight back,don't be pushed around
replace fear with anger
stand your ground.
When the light flooded in
illuminating the scene,
when the danger had gone
then I realised it was only a dream.

TONY MARTIN 29-3-2011

the Darkness of Life

I must return through the darkness of life
into the wilderness of tranquility
leaving behind the fragility
of a torment so blind.
Though this journey will be harduous
filled with regret and humility
commonplace to my kind,
every step must be taken truthfully
along the path back to my own mind.
Through the darkness I see the light
GLOWING
keeping each step firmly on the cloud shrouded path of
honesty and hope,
I must continue to search for the light which
shines through the darkness of life
warming this feeling of cold hatred.
ONE STEP AT A TIME
slowly at first,increase the strength of each new step
as the fragility of tranquility approaches,
forcing away the darkness,soothing the torment,
CARESSING
gently opening up the door
releasing the pressure created by the darkness of life
passing furtively from one mind to the other
always wanting to return to the darkness of life
the only place where comfort reigns
softening the hurt from the brighter side of life,
ANGUISH
suffering through the torment of this struggle between love and hate
BRIGHT LIGHT
heavy darkness somehow softer to me

easing the sentimental memories the suffering brings.
Still the light beckons through the darkness of life,
should I succumb once more to the beauty of this soft
caressing promise or remain in the security of darkness?
TWO MINDS
love and hate battling through the turmoil of this fragile tranquility,
DARKNESS
strength holding me together through the turmoil of these tormented minds,
trying desperately to close the door.
STRUGGLING
please leave me alone
alone to suffer as I must,to decide for myself on which side to close
the door.
TRANQUIL FRAGILITY
blind torment of this hatred of love that burns inside
feeding the darkness of this love for the hatred of the light
drawing me towards the cloud shrouded path forcing apart
these two minds which hold me together,
which create the darkness.
TONIGHT
tomorrow morning these two minds will once again join forces
bringing peace into the brightness of a new day,
release fom the torment,
until once again the darkness of life returns to fight another battle
with the glowing bright light,
these battles become fewer and less frenetic,
which mind do I want to win?
which mind will I allow to win?
These questions I cannot answer
These questions do I want to answer?

TONY MARTIN 19-05-2011.

the Door

From inside it looks
Solid,heavy and
Dark brown
From the outside
Who knows
Even you could push it down.

Tony Martin 1-2-1997

the End

When the final leaf falls from the tree
THEN
You will see.
When the wind breaths her final sigh
THEN
You will know why.
When the clouds release their final drop
THEN
Will you stop.
When the moon turns her final wave
THEN
Your life should I save.
When the tide takes her final grain of sand
THEN
What is left of land.
When the humble bee delivers her final seed
THEN
What will become of greed.
When you have taken all you dare from the majestic steer
THEN
There is no reason to remain here.
When the white dove realises she has wasted all her love
THEN
Will you seek guidance from above.
If you do and I am tired of giving what I can
THEN
Will this be the end of MAN.

TONY MARTIN 22-12-1996

the Flame of Love

by Tony Martin on Mar 3.

Burning brightly
Below the surface of this fragile pool
Lies the flame from your heart
Which you gave to this romantic fool.
Noone saw
Not even your first love
As the arrows of fate from Cupid's bow
Rained down on us from Heaven above.
The heart of the flame
Burning brightly for me
So glorious and strong taking strength from your voice
As you whisper my name.
Noone must know
Of this love that we share
Cupid's arrows were late
But at last they are here.
Beauty surrounds me
Angels gathering above
But through the glow of this flame
All I see is your love.

TONY MARTIN 3-3-2011

the Glory of Fame

by Tony Martin on Nov 17, 2010. © TONY MARTIN, All rights reserved

I need the glory
I must have the fame
At the end of this story
When I return to from where I came
Without this glory I will have no name.

The money you can have
I shall only waste it
As long as I can afford to live
Just enough to taste it.

Look after me
Help me to succeed
When the truth is told
And I have had what I need
Then your blood will run cold
As you watch my heart bleed.

TONY MARTIN 21-1-1997

the Krooked Kitchen

by Tony Martin on May 28.

Uneven floors,
loosely hanging doors,
forever boiling kettle
made from uneven mettle,
shiny used surfaces,noisy fridge,
dirty window ledge.
Cupboards full of secrets
noone left to tell
what happened yesterday,
who knows how lives fray,
shadows remain from the stories of long ago
hidden pain
reflections of shame,
dirty pans
wasted food
stained walls
blood soaked floors,
noone left to see
who locked the doors.
Enter alone,feel the strain
of the anguish caused by the hatred of wasted time,
a time spent sustaining a life created through lust
now returned to everlasting
DUST.

TONY MARTIN 29-05-2011

the Time is Right

by Tony Martin on Jun 5. © TONY MARTIN,

The time is right
it could happen tonight
the feeling overwhelms me
is it necessary to feel such fright
danger exudes
causing fear
not for myself
but anyone who comes near.

The time is right
I must not falter
find the prey
and lead him to the halter.

Enjoy the tension
feel the blood flowing
warm through my veins
increasing the apprehension
of these dangerous games.

The time is right
enjoy the thrill
The time is right
I must take my fill
The time is right
the moment is upon us
The time is right
for me to kill.

TONY MARTIN 4-06-2011

the Whole Truth

by Tony Martin on Feb 18, 2010. © TONY MARTIN,

Such an elusive commodity
never easy to find
seldom believed when heard
so easily distorted
even when spoken sincerely.

Sometimes not easy to accept
even so everyone expects it
to be delivered
never easy to define.

Sometimes eager to be heard
often falls on deaf ears
usually taken out of context
when used to criticise.

Embarrasses politicians when
desperately needed in times of crisis
can be used to frighten
always distorted when used to accuse.

Eventually will be used to save mankind
who have so often distorted the
whole truth in the hope of creating
thier own paradise.

What failures we have been
THAT IS THE WHOLE TRUTH.

AN AFTER THOUGHT
The tragedy of adolescent naivety
created by teenage exuberance
whils't learning of life
through the heartache of puberty.

TONY MARTIN.

to Drown

The dampness now closes in,
Water all around
Below the surface of the sea
For me
There is no sound.

Sharks,Dlphins and Whales
Aimlessly swim by
Talking to each other
BUT
The only thing I need now
IS
The love of my mother.

TONY MARTIN 6-12-1996

to Write With a Brush

If only I could paint
What a picture you would make
A picture paints a thousand words
A thousand words can't lift a brush
It all seems a waste of ink
All I do is think
And write
I wish I could paint
Or draw
Then you would SEE what I think
Of you
To read as I write is not easy I know
Perhaps
I should read it to you
Then perhaps
I would understand too.

TONY MARTIN 16-10-1993
Too Late
All that is left now
are the ashes,
burnt out remnants
of times gone by,
left to go cold
dusty and grey,
devoid of all energy,
too late now for a bright new day.

TONY MARTIN 22-4-2011

Tormented Demons

by Tony Martin on Mar 10, 2010. © TONY MARTIN,

OH,The pain,as once again the darkness descends across my life
Causing a hatred of everything I cherish
Seems this time not so easy to displace,
Just like the rock as it approached the window
Causing me to suffer and seek help,
Then she appeared returning me to face my demons
And banish them to their own torment.

Tormented demons throughout my life,lurking in the back of my mind
Waiting for the right time
Now my mind is so vulnerable there is nothing I can do to stop them taking
over
Tears form inside causing the pain of anguish,my body trembles with
The anger the feeling of helplessness brings
Causing my very soul to swell.

My very being is so afraid of the future,
If I find her again and she accepts me,what do I do
I am not ready yet
But,I crave the reassurance her presence brings
Who is she?
She is the ghost of my past and yet the promise of a future so bright,
She is my nemisis,my very soul
Yet the very thought of her I do fear.

Her presence in my mind is so powerful,so beautiful,so warming
Leaves the feeling of the acceptance of life and what it means
A life which is all things to all men
Yet leaves a feeling of emptiness
Which even a prayer could never fill.

So if this be the end of my fear then so be it
Ready or not I will have to go,
The feeling of fulfillment she offers I will accept.
Could this feeling be the love I have searched for?
If so, welcome
If not I pray she will return me to face my demons once again
And banish them once more to the torment of my subconcious void.

TONY MARTIN

Truthful Relief

by Tony Martin on Nov 17, 2010. © TONY MARTIN, All rights reserved

At the age of three
I knew what would happen to me
At one hundred and five I was still alive
In between these times I witnessed many crimes
So easy now to see why
I allowed your life to pass me by
Greed,Hunger,sometimes Disbelief
These excuses were given
Many times by the jealously driven.
IN THE END THE TRUTH WILL BE SUCH A RELIEF.

JUST A THOUGHT
The experience of lifeis nothing
Without the essence of love.

TONY MARTIN 18-11-2010

Tumbling

by Tony Martin on Mar 7, 2010. © TONY MARTIN,

Daydreams visions of you
Distant thoughts of worlds old and new
Visions of a lifetime spent searching
Finding nothing
Leaving behind the future
Old horizons to view.

Coming home feeling lonely
Back to the start
Still searching
Trying to fill this hole in my heart.

Daydreams visions of you
Tumbling through my mind
Holding back the tears
Old loves trying to find.

Holding back the future
Recreating the past
Looking for a life
Never meant to last.

Possibilities still in this empty heart
For you to return and rescue me
From this life you deserted
Tearing me apart.

TONY MARTIN 17-02-2010

Unwanted Kiss

by Tony Martin on Nov 8, 2010.

Return to me the fever of faith
Weaken this spirit so that once again I may drift
Into the darkness,
For 'twas there I found you,
Have I lost you once again.

The fever once again carries my soul
Slowly through the darkness,
Searching,
So close I feel your love,
Senses awakening,
Through the loneliness I float.

The darkness now fades,
Begins to shine,
Bidding me return to a life that once was mine,
The kiss you offered was I supposed to refuse?
Did you not understand
Your trust was all I tried to use.

The darkness is softer now
Nothing is the same
Yet I am still not certain what I should do
What now is left
Does life continue
Or do I return to be betrayed once again.

TONY MARTIN 30-1-1996

Warm Summer Rain

Imagination running wild
As the warm summer rain
Trickles between lace and skin
Through the valley of love
Drawing sensations from within.
Slowly descending towards the oasis of life
Sensuously approaching,
Over the soft lush undergrowth.
Watched over by loves full moon
Gently your tender back arches
Rubbing across the roughness
Of the damp warm covering of the fallen tree,
The oasis of life now drenched from within
As the warm summer rain caresses your skin
Ecstasy prevails as the two liquids collide
One from the Heavens
The other from inside.
Wash away the pain
Cleanse the lust from within
Open up your soul to the pleasures
Of the warm summer rain.

TONY MARTIN 24-01-2011

Weep Not for Me

by Tony Martin on Jul 26. © TONY MARTIN, All rights reserved

Bloodshot and weeping,
hooded and lifeless
through which all of life is seeping.
Witness to all of life's crimes,
secretly watching
absorbing the truth and the lies,
leaving nothing to chance
through the bad times.
Shedding tears for the pain of man,
longing for the changes to come
bringing salvation and hope,
fulfilling the dream created by the
son of man.

WELL

Well;
bring it on,
whatever you have
I'm still waiting.
Do your worst
nothing will surprise
seen it all before
heard all the lies.
Did my best to break away
sever the ties,
cast aside the robe
nothing more to say.
Cloistered,shackled,
held in limbo for the love of a dream
so many dark corners
echoing the scream.
Towers of stone
castled for safety,
too many lifetimes praying alone
searching for glory through life's frailty.
Oaken doors
brightly coloured windows,
cold stone floors
through all your glory the sorrow shows.

TONY MARTIN 13-7-2011.

When the Talking Ends

Where do we go when the talking ends
Do we become lovers
Or shall we remain friends.

Questions are many
Answers so few
Whatever you see does it please you.

Is there more to what's happening
Than we wish to see
Or are the explanations you give enough for me.

What is it from you you think I need
Doubts from the past
Is it this which sows the bad seed.

You said it would be me
But I knew that could not be true
'Twas so easy to see.

Resolutions just jokes in the mind
Empty words spoken in fun
Enviable ideas drifting on the wind.

'Tis now time to decide
The talking no longer makes sense
And there is no place left to hide.

My decision is made
Predictable I may be
But I am not afraid.

Question me no more
Quiz yourself instead
The answers you need are all in your head.

When the talking ends where DO we go
Shall we become lovers
Or do we remain players in this pointless show.

TONY MARTIN 6-1-1996

Why Oh Why

Clouds of mercy
floating by
passing overhead
destroying this clear blue sky,
silver lining not visible
WHY OH WHY
are the feelings left behind
so empty and risible.

Honesty and endeavour
stand for nothing
sourness is the only flavour,
each envelope arrives
crashing to the floor
REJECTION REJECTION
heartbreaking knowing efforts so forlorn
are all that is left.

A lifetime of toil
asking for nothing not even sustenance,
even the air breathed seems stolen
staring into the sky just wondering
WHY OH WHY
a brave face is no longer possible
stomach feels swollen.

Hatred gathers inside for those in charge
these feelings grow stronger
murderess feelings
HURTING HURTING
insides drowning in the tears that now last longer

painful thoughts destroying a mind once so busy
a mind now too tired to cry
just left wondering
WHY OH WHY.

TONY MARTIN 4-06-2011